THE GINGER NINJA

ShooRayner

Hodder
Children's
Books

A division of Hodder Headline Limited

Copyright © 1995 Shoo Rayner

First published in paperback in 1995 by Hodder Children's Books

This edition published in Great Britain in 2002
by Hodder Children's Books

The right of Shoo Rayner to be identified as the Author
of the Work has been asserted by him in accordance with
the Copyright, Designs and Patents Act 1988.

10 9

A Catalogue record for this book is available
from the British Library

ISBN 0340 61955 4

Printed and bound in Great Britain by
The Guernsey Press Co. Ltd, Channel Isles

Hodder Children's Books
A Division of Hodder Headline Limited
338 Euston Road
London NW1 3BH

Chapter One

Ginger's mum is always in a hurry, so every schoolday morning is a terrible rush. But the first day of term is the worst...

Ginger has to make sure that he gets his breakfast in time.

Before they leave home, Mum
checks Ginger's bag.

✓ Books
✓ Pencils
✓ Eraser
✓ Ruler
✓ Snackbox

(It must be said that Mum puts
together a very tasty snackbox!)

Then she licks
his ears clean...

Oh Mum!

Cleans his
whiskers...

Tut!

Checks that his
paws are clean...

And makes him
blow his nose.

Then they...rush...

All the way to school.

Outside the school gates she checks his bag again (just to be sure) and gives him a great big kiss.

Chapter Two

It was the first day of term. All the other kittens were happy to be back at school and were bursting to tell each other what they had been doing during the holidays.

Ginger may not have been the brainiest kitten in the school, but he was probably the happiest. As he settled down at his desk he thought of all the nice things that he could look forward to this term.

MISS TIFFANY

He liked his teacher.

He liked his lessons.
(He liked counting fish best)

He liked singing in the choir.

He loved playing Pawball.

He liked the lunches that
his mum packed for him.

And, most of all,
he liked all his school-friends.

Chapter Three

Miss Tiffany read out their names
from the register.

Ginger

Daisy

Muncher

Hilda

Wilson A.

Wilson D.

Tiddles

"TIDDLES?" called out the
whole class.

They all looked round to see the new kitten – and gasped.

Lurking at the back of the classroom was the largest, stripy kitten they had ever seen. He didn't look very pleased to be there.

After class they tried to make friends with Tiddles but he was not in the mood.

Ginger thought that Tiddles was not a very nice kitten. On the way home he asked his friends what they thought of him.

But Tiddles was not all right....

By the second week of term he
had made friends with the Wilson
twins.

Next came Muncher Matthews.

Soon he had made a lot of friends.

They set up their headquarters behind the bike shed.

The 'Soldiers' would sneakily grab little kittens during break time and march them off to see Tiddles who would make them hand over the contents of their snack boxes.

By the
following
week,
every
breaktime,
there would
be a long
queue
of kittens
stretching
around the
bike shed
and into the
playground.

Ginger knew exactly what was going on but he pretended that he didn't. He wondered when it would be his turn. It wasn't long before Tiddles spotted him and shouted across the playground.

Tiddles prodded Ginger with his paw. It hurt.

Tiddles put on his sickliest grin. Ginger could feel his legs turn all wobbly.

Chapter Four

Ginger's mum was really pleased that Ginger wanted more fishybix to take to school.

He told her that he shared them with his friends and that they all said what a really great cook she was.

It's so nice to know that your friends have such good taste!

Hmmm.

Ginger got quieter and quieter,
and sadder and sadder.
He wanted to tell his mum and
dad what was happening but he
didn't know how to.

Ginger couldn't tell his teachers what was going on because he guessed what Tiddles would do.

Ginger, who had always been
such a happy little kitten
looked sad.

His fur went
all sticky.

His whiskers
drooped.

His tail wouldn't stand up
properly.

He felt very lonely. He thought
he had no one left to talk to.

Chapter Five

One night Ginger's mum and dad were going out to a dance where Mum worked. Grandad came round to babysit.

Ginger loved his grandad. He was always full of stories.

Ginger and Grandad made some supper first.

They played some games for a while.

Then Grandad tried to help with Ginger's homework.

Pretty soon it was time for bed.
Grandad read loads of stories
until he thought Ginger was
fast asleep.

Grandad couldn't help feeling
that Ginger was not a happy
kitten.

Then he heard a noise.

He crept upstairs and listened
at Ginger's door.

Ginger poured out the
whole story.

He told him about Tiddles and
the fishybix and how the other
kittens in Tiddles's gang called
him names.

Titch... Rusty-musty...
Copper-knob... Tangerine...
Orange-Utang...
They say: Knock knock!
Who's there? Orange.
Orange who?
Orange you glad
you're not
Ginger!

Grandad laughed.

Is that all?
They used to
say those things
when I was a
young kitten.

Then Grandad told Ginger all the names that he'd been called as a young, ginger tom.

The Ginger biscuit,

The Gingerbread cat,

Rusty,

Chapter Six

Grandad got something out of his
pocket. He handled it like a
necklace but it was invisible!
He put it carefully around
Ginger's neck.

The time has come to tell you the old family secrets of Gingerness that my Grandfather told me and his Grandfather told before him.

But Grandad, there's nothing there!

That night Ginger slept well and
had exciting dreams.

The next morning Ginger went
straight through the school gates
and walked casually past
Tiddles's gang, who
were leaning up
against a wall.

At break-time Tiddles came
looking for his fishybix.

Inside Ginger knew he was
invincible. He was
the Ginger Ninja!

At dinner-time Tiddles came
looking for Ginger again.

No one had ever spoken to
Tiddles like that. He didn't
know what to do.

After school Tiddles was waiting
for Ginger.

Poor Tiddles was very confused.

Chapter Seven

Next day, Tiddles and his whole gang were waiting for Ginger. Tiddles called across the playground.

The whole school was watching
as Ginger calmly walked past,
ignoring Tiddles and his gang.

Calmly, Ginger took his collar off,

wrapped it round his head

and walked up to Tiddles.

You're a great big, steaming bully!

Duh!

A deathly hush settled
on the playground.

They stared each other out for exactly four minutes and twenty seven seconds. Hardly anyone breathed.

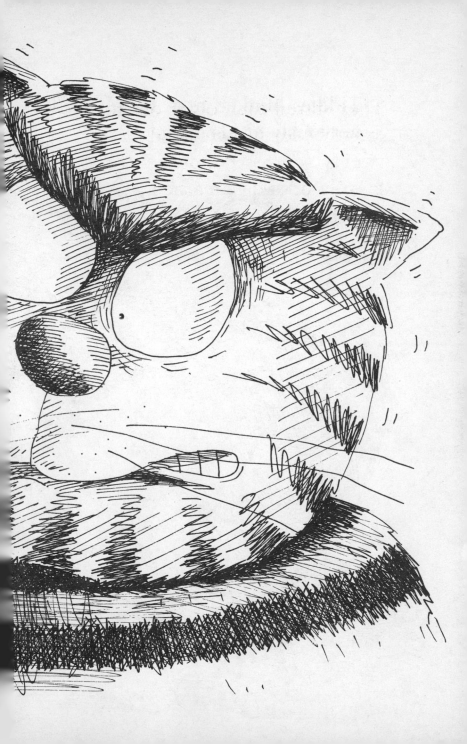

Tiddles blinked first. He glanced nervously at his gang.

Ginger sucked in an almighty
breath and stuck his fur out until
he looked twice his normal size.

Suddenly he let rip at the top
of his voice.

He scared the life out of Tiddles.

The whole school joined in.

Tiddles and his gang ran away to look for somewhere to hide until their mums came to collect them.

Ginger was a hero.

Chapter Eight

Ginger became the most popular
kitten in the school.

His whiskers
straightened up,

his nose
glistened,

and his
eyes started
shining again.

The little kittens saw Ginger as their protector.

Once again, Ginger was the happiest, the proudest...and the loudest kitten in the school.